AMY The Story of a Deaf Child

by Lou Ann Walker
photographs by Michael Abramson

LODESTAR BOOKS   E. P. DUTTON   NEW YORK

LIBRARY OF CONGRESS CATALOGING IN PUBLICATION DATA

Walker, Lou Ann.
    Amy, the story of a deaf child.

    "Lodestar books."
    Bibliography: p.
    Summary: Text and photographs depict the life of deaf
fifth-grader Amy Rowley, who goes to a regular school
and enjoys normal activities with the help of hearing
aids and sign language.
    1. Children, Deaf—Case studies—Juvenile literature.
[1. Deaf.   2. Physically handicapped.   3. Rowley, Amy]
I. Abramson, Michael, ill.   II. Title.
HV2392.W35   1985   362.4'2'0924   [B]   84-21152
ISBN 0-525-67145-5

Published in the United States by E. P. Dutton,
a division of Penguin Books USA Inc.

Published simultaneously in Canada by
Fitzhenry & Whiteside Limited, Toronto

Editor: Virginia Buckley   Designer: Riki Levinson

Printed in the U.S.A.
10 9 8 7 6 5 4

for Speeder

LOU ANN WALKER

for my mother, Frieda Belsky Abramson

MICHAEL ABRAMSON

for my brother, John

AMY ROWLEY

About Amy

When Amy Rowley was about fifteen months old, her mother noticed that she was a very quiet baby. She didn't talk the way her brother, John, had. Her mother and father took her to an audiologist for an examination, and the audiologist found out that Amy was deaf. Nobody knows how it happened. But Amy's mother and father knew exactly how to teach her to talk. They are both deaf themselves.

Now Amy is in fifth grade. She is the only deaf person in her school. Amy wears hearing aids and can lip-read. All during kindergarten, first grade, and second grade, Amy's mother went over her schoolwork with her for several hours each evening.

Amy's mother and father wanted her to have the same educational opportunities as nonhandicapped children. They also wanted a full-time interpreter for her, to which they felt she was entitled under federal law. So they took the case to court, and the lower courts agreed; Amy did have an interpreter in the third and fourth grades, and her classwork improved greatly. Then the

Supreme Court reversed the decision. Amy could no longer have an interpreter in that school.

You see, even though Amy is deaf, she is just like every eleven-year-old. Amy collects stamps, reads many, many books, and has lots of friends. She may not be able to understand a program on television, but she can make up in her mind what it's about by watching the pictures. She probably works twice as hard—no, probably ten times as hard—as others to talk and make her words sound like everybody else's.

Amy can be funny and silly, and if she has to, she can be serious. She is almost never sad. She makes adjustments by using many special devices. She says she wouldn't want to change anything in her life. Amy is very happy being normal and doing some things differently.

At the end of this book are a series of photographs showing Amy signing and a list of resources for readers who would like more information.

As you can see, I love to climb trees. I also like to take care of my pets—my rabbit Brown Eyes, my cat Checkers, and my parakeet Garfield. Also my fish. If you look closely at this picture, you can see my hearing aid. My mom and dad are deaf, too. My brother John is hearing. He's thirteen. I'm eleven.

In the mornings, my alarm clock has a flashing light to wake me up. I like it better when my mom comes to get me out of bed.

Our house also has lights that flash when someone rings the doorbell.

Sometimes when I'm being lazy, I can talk my mom
into helping me put on my shoes. She says, "Oh, Amy!"

I can hear myself talking right now. I can hear some
sounds, but I can't understand everything. Say I heard an
ambulance go by. I wouldn't know what it was unless I
saw it.

This is me with my neighbor Carolyn. We play basketball together, and sometimes we just play around the neighborhood.

Carolyn likes to play hide-and-seek. And we can play it two different ways.

I'm the fastest runner of the girls in my class.

I think I talk two languages: sign language and spoken language. Kids like me to teach them signs. I'm making an *R*, but Carolyn is making a *G*. So I point at my fingers to show her the right way to do it.

We are finger spelling the alphabet. Carolyn is making a *C*. I'm making a *D*. At home we don't finger spell each letter of a word. That takes too long! We mostly use signs. If a word or a name doesn't have a sign, then we spell it out.

My brother, John, is very sporty. He likes to go swimming; play basketball, football, baseball, and lacrosse; and do track. All the sports he likes, I do too, but not as much as he does.

One thing I like about being deaf is that I don't have to do as many errands or make as many phone calls as my brother, John, does. If I were hearing, my parents would depend on me more, because they're deaf.

A couple of times in school, kids made fun of me. John took my side. He told them I'm just as good as they are. He got so mad, I was afraid he was going to beat them up. They stopped making fun of me.

That's some brother, my brother John.

One thing I feel bad about, though. When my family was on television once, Johnny was cut out of the picture—and he was sitting right next to my mother! I don't want to leave John out of anything.

This is my rabbit, Brown Eyes. He's a very soft rabbit.
He doesn't make any noise.
Sometimes he gets away.

Checkers knows we're deaf. He comes to get us when he wants to go out, and he doesn't meow if just Mom and Dad and I are around. He meows only when he sees John. I like to hold my hand over his throat to feel the vibrations while he's purring.

I'm pretending to sign to one of the teddy bears in my bedroom. But most of the time I'd rather be outside playing with my live pets.

I have a garden in the backyard, where I grow radishes. The mint leaves we grow are good to chew on.

Last year I sent away for daisy seeds through a Girl Scout magazine. I planted them, but it was after the expiration date. They didn't grow at all during the summer, and I forgot about them. But then they grew this year. I was surprised!

One day after the flowers came up, Mom asked me to go get the pruner. I said, "What's that for? Prunes? I want to cut flowers, not prunes!" I was kidding her.

That's my dad helping me decide what else to plant.

I'm typing on a TTY—a teletypewriter-telephone. It helps deaf people telephone each other. You put the receiver of a phone onto the top of the TTY, type your message, and the words flash out on a tiny screen like the one on a calculator. The words appear on your and the other person's TTYs at the same time.

After you finish a message on the TTY, you type *GA.* That means "go ahead"; it tells the other person to start typing a reply. To say good-bye, you type *SK,* which means "stop keying."

When our phone rings at home, special lights—different from the doorbell lights—flash on, so that we know to answer the phone. Because it's portable, we can take the TTY on trips and make phone calls to deaf friends from a phone booth anywhere.

Mom likes to help me fix my hair before I go to school. If she pulls and it hurts, I yell "Ow!" Mom used to help me a lot with my homework, especially before I had an interpreter in the third grade. My mom is a real whiz brain.

All the other kids who go to my school are hearing. I'm the only deaf person at Furnace Woods School.

When I'm in school, I wear a body aid: a big hearing aid that fits on my belt. My teachers wear microphones that send signals to the body aid.

This is Mr. Smelter, one of my teachers. He is helping me with math. That's one of the hardest subjects for me.

Reading lips helps me understand what people are saying. But I can't really understand the noises I hear from my body aid without looking at people's mouths.

If I can't figure out what the teacher is saying, I ask "What?" Then he repeats it, and I look closer at his mouth. I probably say "What?" more than most people do, but I want to know everything that is going on. Sometimes kids don't understand what I say, and so I have to repeat myself, too.

Some people shout at me. They think I'll be able to hear them better. It's harder to understand them, though, because shouting makes their mouths look strange so that I can't even lip-read.

School isn't too hard for me. My favorite subjects are reading, English, and P.E.

Here we're trying to figure out the answer to a mathematics problem. I couldn't believe the answer!

My friends and I pass notes to each other in class. Also, we made up a game. It's similar to charades. And a few of my friends can sign. One girl made up her own signs.

I help other kids in school, and they help me too, especially if I don't understand what the teacher says.

I used to have an interpreter, but not anymore. Kids in my school liked the interpreter. She was good at helping them. She was like a teacher's aide. I miss having an interpreter, because I found work easier with one.

At recess we have girls' teams and boys' teams. When they bother us, we beat up the boys and they leave.

Mostly I like the swings and the obstacle course.

I bring my own lunch. I like to eat a lot, but I don't like school food. My mother says I'm fussy.

In P.E., I'd rather do sports than watch the coach's mouth.

When the coach blows the whistle, the sound through the hearing aid hurts my ears. It's like a squeal.

Three times a week I go by myself to see the speech teacher, Mrs. Pasierb. While she talks, she writes on the blackboard and shows me how to say the words. Then she has me feel her throat so that I can understand how to make the sounds she makes. Some deaf kids learn to make certain sounds by holding a feather or a balloon in front of their lips.

One hour a day I go to see the teacher for the deaf, Mrs. Annis. She travels to different schools in my district. Mrs. Annis checks to see if my hearing aid is working, and she talks about how I'm doing in my subjects. She gives me homework, just like my speech teacher does. I'd rather stay in the classroom with the rest of the kids than have so many special teachers.

After school I usually have a lot of homework to do, but I try to get it done right away so that I can read some books.

People keep asking me what I want to be when I grow up. I don't really know. I might become a teacher like my mom or a research chemist like my father. Or I might become something else.

After school is out for the day, Mom and Dad sometimes take me to the Furnace Woods playground. Usually there aren't any other kids there. It's just us.

Even when I'm outside, my mom tells me "Shhh" if I make too much noise.

Mom and Dad like being outdoors. It's probably because they like sports so much. Once every four years, deaf people from all over the world compete in the Deaf Olympics. My mom and dad were both Deaf Olympic swimmers.

People have to stand somewhat far apart when they are signing, so that they can see what other people are saying.

My dad is so cute. He's a softie.

That's my friend Suzie with me. She's teaching me to skateboard. I taught her some signs. In the picture below, she's saying "meet."

Suzie's family, the Schoenigs, have a neat tire swing.
That's Suzie's brother we're swinging.

If Suzie wants to talk with me and she's standing beside me or behind me, she has to tap my shoulder to get my attention.

On Mother's Day the whole family got dressed up. Mom wears a hearing aid just like mine behind her ear.

Mom gave me a kiss for her presents. And when she read Dad's card, she gave him a kiss too. We gave her a vase and some flowers.

After we had breakfast and Mom opened her presents, we went to church. We go to Saint Augustine's Episcopal Church. It's a long drive.

We like to go to Saint Augustine's because the church has an interpreter, Marion. That's Marion and Father Wayne with me.

During the service I like to sing. It helps if someone points out the words as we go along.

Last year I sang with the fourth- and fifth-grade glee club at school. I had an interpreter for singing. The interpreter signed the words in time with the music, so that I could see the rhythm of the songs.

Father Wayne is always nice to me and likes to talk after church. Sometimes he tries to sign with my family. He also has a TTY so he can call our house and we can call him.

This is my friend Nancy Hlibok with me. She's deaf too. But her whole family is deaf, even her three brothers. Nancy is a ballerina. She feels the beat of the music through the floor.

When she comes over to my house, we like to do somersaults.

In my backyard we put up a tent so that Nancy and I could sleep outside overnight. We had to bring in a light so that we could see each other's signs. (Also, we didn't want to get scared.)

For a while I thought I would like to go to school in New York City with my deaf friends. But New York is too far to go everyday from where we live, and I wouldn't want to live away from home.

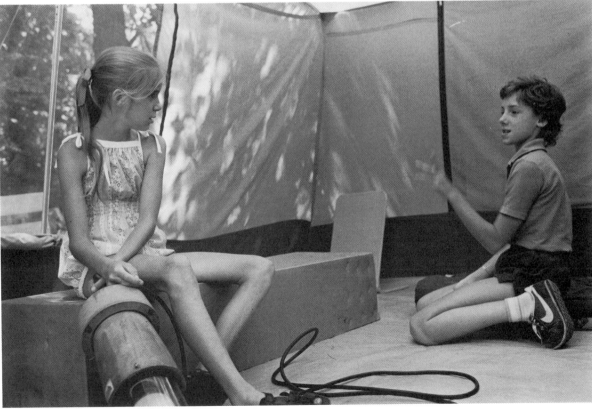

Here I am with some more of my friends—Claudia Fraenkel, Debbie Bravin, and that's Nancy on the right end. We all have deaf parents. Claudia is the only hearing one among the four of us. Because her mom and dad are deaf, it's easy for her to talk to us.

When you sign, you have to move your face a lot. It's called being expressive. It helps people understand you better.

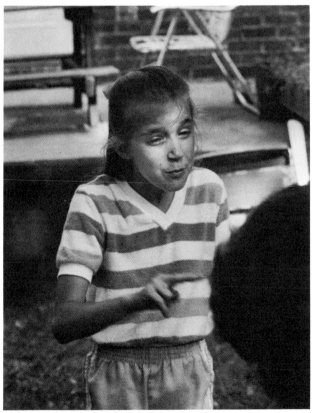

    While our parents are talking in sign language, the four of us are playing. I decided we could make a kind of obstacle course out of lawn chairs.

    After that we went to get ice cream. If I'm in a restaurant or someplace and someone can't figure out what I want, then I can always point. Or if the person really can't understand me and John is there, he interprets.

Today at school I took out five books. My mother asked me how I was going to finish all those books before I left on vacation. I told her I'd try.

There's a public library near my house. My mom drives John and me there. I have three favorite authors—three *P*'s—Peggy Parish, Daniel Pinkwater, and Robert Peck. Also E. B. White. I love *The Trumpet of the Swan* and *Stuart Little*.

Every summer the library posts a reading contest on the bulletin board. A boat with my name on it sails to a port every time I read a certain number of books. Right now I'm on my second voyage. Last year I got a special ice-cream coupon for winning.

That's Yoda, from *The Empire Strikes Back,* behind me at the library. By the way, we get to see captioned movies at home. The words people are saying are printed at the bottom of the screen. The captions even tell when someone coughs or laughs or when music is playing. I think captioned movies have helped me read better. I guess you could say I've been reading the movies since I was a really little kid.

I also like to watch cartoons. Even if I don't understand the words, the pictures make sense to me. That's because I make up for myself what the show is about. Say there's a mouse and a football. The mouse falls in the ocean and his wife lives by a football. I make up a story about how the mouse gets back to his wife, and I watch the cartoon to see what happens. Sometimes I write my own stories.

Two years ago, Mom and Dad went to the National Association of the Deaf convention. That's what NAD on my tee shirt stands for.

My tee shirt says: My folks went to the NAD Convention in Cincinnati and all they brought me back was this ~~crumy~~ crummy tee shirt!

Sometimes after we go to the library, I talk Mom into taking John and me to our neighbor's pool to swim. That's one of my favorite things to do. Of course I don't wear my hearing aids in the water.

Lots of hearing people ask me what it's like to be deaf, but I never ask them what it's like to be hearing.

I think deafness feels like peace. Hearing people have to hear all sorts of things they don't want to hear. I don't.

More About Amy

At the end of the summer, Amy went to South Carolina to visit her cousins. (She did finish reading the five library books before she left.)

In September, she and her family moved to Mountain Lakes, New Jersey, a town about thirty miles from New York City. The house they moved into didn't have a doorbell, so they rigged one up with a light that flashes on and off, just like the one in their former house.

Some deaf children are shy, but Amy is not. She says she made approximately twenty-one new friends the first day at her new school. Now Amy and John have even more sports activities than before.

The teachers in Amy's new school saw that she was having difficulty with science, social studies, and math; so the school district hired three interpreters to come in on different days of the week for those subjects. Otherwise, Amy says she's perfectly happy. Lots of the kids in her new school have asked her to teach them signs or finger spelling, and she says she's learning things from them, too.

grow; spring (the season)	dog	cat
bear	rabbit	squirrel
lion	spider	bird

Wow!	funny	sad
I	love	you
taking pictures	yawn	Time out!

Resources

Communications

Broadcaster
National Association of the Deaf
814 Thayer Avenue
Silver Spring, Maryland 20910

Deaf American
National Association of the Deaf
814 Thayer Avenue
Silver Spring, Maryland 20910

National Captioning Institute
5203 Leesburg Pike
Suite 1500
Falls Church, Virginia 22041
> Sends out information about television closed captioning. (To obtain closed captioning, deaf people purchase a special decoding device which allows them to see subtitles on some regularly scheduled television programs.)

Registry of Interpreters for the Deaf, Inc.
Gallaudet College
Washington, D.C. 20002
> Can provide lists of qualified professional oral and sign language interpreters and information about how to use an interpreter.

Sign Language Programs
Gallaudet College
Washington, D.C. 20002
> Can direct you to sign language classes in your area. Gallaudet is the only liberal arts college for deaf people in the world.

Silent News
343 Forest Avenue
Paramus, New Jersey 07652
> A newspaper for and about deaf people.

Special Materials Project
814 Thayer Avenue
Silver Spring, Maryland 20910
   Can provide information about captioned films.

Telecommunications for the Deaf, Inc.
814 Thayer Avenue
Silver Spring, Maryland 20910
   Can provide information on TTYs.

Education

American Society for Deaf Children, Inc.
(formerly, International Association of Parents of the Deaf)
814 Thayer Avenue
Silver Spring, Maryland 20910
   An organization for parents who have deaf children. The group
   publishes a newsletter.

General

National Center for Law and the Deaf
7th Street and Florida Avenue, N.E.
Washington, D.C. 20002
   Has information on Amy's Supreme Court case, as well as other
   legal information about deaf people.

Books

Bornstein, Harry. *The Signed English Dictionary*. Washington,
   D.C.: Gallaudet College Press, 1975.
Charlip, Remy and Mary Beth. *Handtalk: An ABC of Finger Spell-
   ing and Sign Language*. New York: School Book Service,
   1974.
Costello, Elaine. *Signing: How To Speak With Your Hands*. New
   York: Bantam, 1983.
Michel, Anna. *The Story of Nim: The Chimp Who Learned Lan-
   guage*. New York: Alfred A. Knopf, 1980.
Rosenberg, Maxine B. *My Friend Leslie: The Story of a Handi-
   capped Child*. New York: Lothrop, Lee & Shepard Books, 1983.